KLAUS BLIESENER

An Almost Perfect Robbery

KLAUS BLIESENER

The Ace Detectives

An Almost Perfect Robbery

containing
Smugglers on the Ferry
and **An Almost Perfect Robbery**

A Magnet Book

This Magnet paperback edition
First published in Great Britain 1986
by Methuen Children's Books Ltd
11 New Fetter Lane, London EC4P 4EE
First published in West Germany 1984
as Schmuggler auf der Fähre
Copyright © 1984 Otto Maier Verlag Ravensburg
English translation copyright © 1986 Anthea Bell
Printed in Great Britain

ISBN 0 416 54970 5

A ferry was slowly making its way into the little harbour of Northey Island. It was full of passengers going to Northey for a holiday, and among them were the three Ace Detectives. Of course, they didn't know yet that they were going to earn that name.

The children's real name was Williams. Sarah was the youngest. She was actually called Sandy, because she had sandy hair. Then there was Robert, who had an enigmatic smile (like the famous Mona Lisa). Robert had a passion for little black notebooks, and was hardly ever seen without one. And Alan, the eldest, had sandy hair too, but his nickname was Conker, because he was conkers champion of his class at school.

All the children were looking forward to their holiday very much. And it was to turn out much, much more exciting than they had expected, as you'll soon see.

You can help the three children in their detective work too. Keep a pencil handy – you'll be needing it from time to time.

So have a good time with the Ace Detectives!

Smugglers on the Ferry

1 Sandy, Robert and Conker were standing by the rail of the ferry. The crossing from the mainland had taken almost an hour, and it had been a little rough. The children couldn't wait to feel solid ground underfoot again.

'Look, there's the harbour at last,' said Sandy.

'And about time too!' said Robert. 'I can't wait to get down to the beach!'

'We must go to the boarding house first,' said Mr and Mrs Williams. 'It's called the Dunes. You children can help us carry the cases, and then we'll ask about the beach and the rest of the island. All right?'

But the children didn't answer. They had just noticed a packet of cigarettes lying on deck. 'A full packet, too,' said Sandy. 'It hasn't been opened. There's such a crowd here – I wonder who can have lost it?'

'Give it to Dad,' suggested Robert.

'No, we'll give it straight back to its owner,' said Conker. 'Let's go and find him. It shouldn't take too long.'

Robert grinned, nudged him, and pointed to someone in the crowd. 'It didn't!' he said. 'I've done it already! I bet that's the person who lost the cigarette packet!'

Have a good look at all the people.
Only one of them is really likely to have lost the
cigarette packet. Who is it?

2 The man in white trousers whom Robert had spotted was still looking out to sea. Sandy cleared her throat. 'Excuse me!' she said, in a friendly way. The man turned round. 'I think you've lost this,' she went on, showing him the packet of cigarettes. 'There's another packet about to fall out of your trouser pocket any moment, too.'

The man felt his trouser pocket in alarm, and then snatched the packet Sandy was holding. 'Give me that!' he snapped. 'Okay, kids, clear out!'

'Well, what a nasty, rude man!' said Sandy, indignantly. 'We were only trying to be helpful!'

'He certainly is rather peculiar,' agreed Robert. 'Look at him now – anxiously watching all his luggage.'

'Yes, as if he thought someone was going to chuck it overboard!' grinned Conker.

Suddenly there was a jolt. Conker almost fell over Robert. The *Seal* had reached the pier and stopped, her engines rumbling. The passengers were scurrying about excitedly. 'Let's wait a moment, children!' said Mrs Williams. 'We'll let other people get off the boat first.'

The three children watched the passengers disembarking. Suddenly Robert got his notebook out. 'That unfriendly man's just gone on shore – I might as well note it down.'

'That's not a note, it's a drawing of a seagull,' said Conker, looking at Robert's sketch. 'What's the idea?'

'Well, you could say he's leaving by seagull!' said Robert, smiling.

'Where is he?' asked Sandy. 'Oh yes – I can see him now!'

 Take a look at Robert's drawing, and then you ought to be able to find the man too. Where is he?

8

3 The man was just riding off past the big clock on a bicycle with a big carrier, the kind used for deliveries, with a picture of a seagull on it.

A few days later, when the children were having breakfast at The Dunes, Conker noticed a circular issued by the Northey Island police hanging over the sideboard. 'I say, that reminds me of the man on the ferry!' said Robert with interest, when he had read the circular too. He was thinking so hard that when he reached for a bread roll, he took a handful of marmalade instead. Sandy giggled. Conker grinned, and then said, thoughtfully, 'You mean because he made such a fuss over those cigarettes of his?'

Robert nodded, and looked at the drawing in his notebook again. 'We might look for him, in case he's a smuggler,' he suggested. 'We could start by trying to track down the bike with the gull on it.'

'What nonsense you children do talk!' said Mr Williams, burying himself in his newspaper.

Sandy whispered something to her mother, and then hurried out of the dining room. 'Come on!' she told the others. 'I've had an idea.'

The nice woman in the tourist office told them the names of five hotels, all of which had the word 'gull' somewhere in them. ' ... and finally, The Silvery Seagull,' said Robert, writing it down.

Conker was getting impatient. 'Right, let's go!' he said. But all of a sudden he stopped short, and dug Robert in the ribs. 'Oh, I see another name you could write down too!' he told him.

 Take a good look at the picture, and you'll see the name of another gull. This sixth gull even has a first name. What is it?

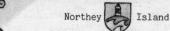

Northey **Island** Island

WARNING!

Reports have been received that tax-free
cigarettes are being offered for sale on
Northey Island.   These cigarettes bear the
brand name NICCO.   There is no duty stamp
on the packets.

Please note that tax-free goods may not be
sold on Northey.   Any information about
these cigarettes would be welcomed by the

NORTHEY ISLAND POLICE

4 'P-E-T-E-R G-U-L-L,' Sandy read out aloud. You could see the name written downwards on a board hanging on the wall behind the counter.

The five hotels were a long way apart, so it took the three children almost the whole morning to check them all. 'And they all had delivery bicycles,' said Robert, summing up the results of their investigations. 'Two didn't have seagulls painted on the bikes, and the other three did have pictures of gulls, but not the same as the one I sketched in my notebook.'

'So that just leaves Peter Gull,' said Conker.

Sandy saw the shop as soon as they turned into the little pedestrian precinct. Conker and Robert were about to go straight in, but Sandy said, 'Wait a moment! We don't need to go in at all. Come over here!' And she knelt down by a gate leading into a yard. The gate was closed, but you could see through a knot-hole in the wood.

'The bike!' cried Robert and Conker together.

They opened the gate and hurried into the yard. Robert inspected the bicycle and compared the seagull pictures. 'It's just the same,' he said, triumphantly.

'But suppose there's another bike like this one?' said Conker.

'We could always ask Mr Gull,' said Sandy. She climbed up on some old crates and peered through a window pane. 'My word!' she cried in surprise. 'Come and have a look at this! Another clue pointing to our man on the ferry!'

Can you spot Sandy's clue as well? You've seen two of it before! What is it?

12

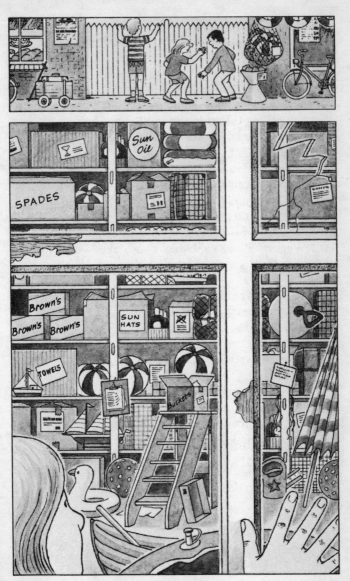

5 Yes, there it was: one of the two suitcases the stranger had been guarding so jealously. 'Come on!' said Conker. 'We'll go into the shop and pretend we want to buy something.'

'But suppose Mr Gull himself is the man we're after?' said Sandy. She breathed a sigh of relief when she saw the man selling things in the shop. They had never seen him before. Luckily he was busy with other customers, so they had a chance to look round.

'Yes, it's Mr Gull all right!' whispered Sandy, who had boldly made her way right past the stout little man and back to the others. 'He's got his name on his overall.'

'So the man on the ferry isn't Peter Gull, anyway,' said Conker under his breath.

'I wonder if we've made a mistake?' said Robert thoughtfully. 'I know the bike's in the yard – but have you seen so much as a single cigarette here? I haven't!'

'No, I haven't either,' Sandy admitted. 'Oh, watch out – here he comes!'

'Well, and what can I do for you?' asked Mr Gull, giving the children a friendly look over his glasses.

'Er – have you – um – got any cigarettes?' Conker stammered.

Mr Gull frowned. 'You mean chocolate cigarettes, I hope?' he said suspiciously. Robert hastily nodded. 'No, I'm afraid I don't sell sweets, only things for the beach: buckets and spades and so on. See for yourselves!'

'Yes, I see. Thank you very much,' said Robert, politely. But he winked at Sandy and Conker, and whispered, 'Mr Gull seems to like puzzles! Come on, let's go.'

You can probably see something puzzling in the shop too. Decode the message. What does it say?

6 'You just have to cross out or change the letters of each word corresponding to the numbers given,' Robert explained. 'And then the picture code on Mr Gull's notice above the sailing ships says "beach kiosks".'

'Well done, Robert!' said Sandy.

'Let's go down to the beach, then,' said Conker, starting off at a trot.

They soon saw the kiosk on the promenade. Conker bought three strawberry ices. 'And a packet of Nicco cigarettes, please,' added Robert.

They watched with bated breath as the sales assistant took a cigarette packet off the shelf and pushed it over the counter. 'That'll be two pounds twenty-five,' he said.

'Oh dear – I'm afraid we've only brought two pounds with us,' Sandy pretended. She nudged Conker, who got the idea and pushed the packet back again, pocketing his change from the ices.

'Well, so he *does* sell Nicco cigarettes,' said Robert, taking the wrapping off his ice. 'And all the packets have duty stamps on them, as far as I could see. On the other hand, he may be selling the duty-free cigarettes under the

counter ... '

'But he'd be careful not to let everyone know, with the police after him,' said Conker. Suddenly he stopped short. 'Didn't the code say beach *kiosks*? There's another of Mr Gull's kiosks over there!'

Have a good look at the promenade. Where is the second kiosk?

7 Once the seagulls had all flown by, the children could see the kiosk easily. 'Though if we don't get any farther than last time ... ' muttered Robert.

'Do we buy ices again?' asked Sandy, throwing the crumpled wrapper of her last ice into a litter bin.

'We don't have to,' said Conker, 'and anyway, we can't! Look, the kiosk's closed.'

'Back soon,' Robert read. 'The sales assistant's had to go out.'

'Then we can have a good look!' said Conker. He pressed his nose against the glass window to look at what was for sale inside the kiosk.

'We're getting nowhere,' sighed Robert. 'Perfectly ordinary cigarettes with a duty stamp on them. They've even put the police circular up too!'

'Let's go down to the beach until the kiosk opens,' suggested Conker.

But when they came back to the kiosk, about ten minutes later, it was still closed. 'What does he mean, back soon?' said Sandy, crossly. 'There still isn't anybody here.'

'I think you're wrong,' whispered Conker, mysteriously.

For a moment Sandy didn't know what he meant. Then she understood. 'You're right,' she said. 'Someone's been in the kiosk since we were here before.'

 Look at the two pictures very carefully. What is the difference between them?

8 Sure enough, somebody must have been in the kiosk, because the notice was now standing propped against the window. Conker signed to the others to be quiet a moment. 'Music!' he whispered. 'Coming from round the back.' They made a wide detour around the kiosk, and then ducked down under a wild rose bush.

'My word!' whispered Sandy. 'The man on the ferry!'

'So it is!' Conker agreed. He looked inquiringly at Robert. 'Does that brilliant notebook of yours say if the cigarette packet we picked up on the boat had a duty stamp or not?'

'No,' said Robert. 'I didn't know it was important, at the time.'

'We must wait here and try to find out if the man knows anything about the smuggled cigarettes,' said Sandy, and Conker nodded.

They waited in the shelter of the rose bush, and five minutes later their patience was rewarded. 'He's going back into the kiosk at last,' said Conker. 'I'll see if I can find anything where he was sitting.' Two minutes later he came scuttling back and dropped into the grass beside Robert and Sandy again. 'Well, no cigarette ends or empty packets – but I did find this!' And Conker dropped some torn scraps of crumpled paper into the palm of one hand. It didn't take long to put the pieces together again.

'Well, look at that!' said Robert. 'Our friend of the ferry doesn't seem to have liked this news item much!'

You can probably guess what those scraps of paper said when they were put together. What was it?

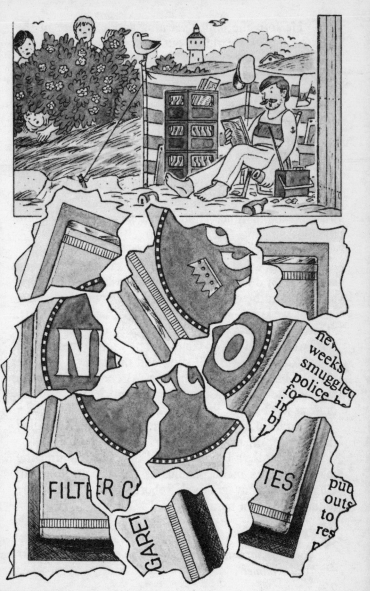

N O

new
weeks
smuggled
police b
fo
in
b

FILTER C

GARET

TES

put
outs
to
res

9 'He tore the police warning and a picture of the smuggled cigarettes out of the newspaper,' said Conker. 'I wonder why? After all, there must be lots of copies of the paper with that picture in it on the island. How funny!'

'At least it shows he *is* interested in the cigarettes in some way,' said Robert.

'But now what?' asked Sandy, baffled.

'Now we watch him!' said Robert, making a few more notes in his notebook.

They spent the rest of the afternoon within sight of the kiosk – and within earshot too. Nothing at all happened for quite a long time. Then, at last, someone came up to the kiosk, saying, 'Hi there, Pearce!'

The three children watched with bated breath.

'Same as usual, please,' said the customer, putting some money down. The man in the kiosk said something in reply, but the children couldn't make out what it was.

'Still, we know our man's name is Pearce,' said Robert. 'That's worth the wait!'

'Careful!' whispered Conker. The window at the front of the kiosk was banged shut, and then they heard the clink of bottles round at the back. A couple of minutes later all the goods on display had been cleared, and the door at the back of the kiosk was locked.

'He's closing!' said Sandy in surprise, as they watched the man set off towards the Spa hotel.

'After him!' said Conker. And they hurried after the man, being as inconspicuous as they could about it. Conker suddenly grabbed Robert's arm. 'I know the initial of his first name!' he said.

 What is the only possible initial for the man's first name?

10 There was a letter H on the man's key-ring. Robert immediately pulled out his notebook, and almost fell over. 'It's not very easy, writing while you're walking along,' he said.

'And it wasn't very easy finding you children, either,' said a familiar voice behind them all of a sudden.

All three children stopped dead. Of course – their parents! They'd forgotten all about them.

'We thought you were just going to look in at the tourist office – and here we find you slinking along the promenade as if you were on the warpath or something!' said Mr Williams, not sounding very pleased.

'Well, we're actually following a suspect,' Conker tried to explain.

'You kids and your nonsense! Well, you'll just have to go on following your suspect tomorrow,' said Mr Williams, laughing.

That evening Robert came bursting into the room where the others were sitting with the telephone directory. 'Looks as if our friend's on the phone too,' he said. 'At least, there are seven people called Pearce here. Two of them seem to be women, and the rest are men.'

'And one begins with an H,' Sandy pointed out. 'Henry Pearce, 12 Furze Road.'

Conker unfolded a map of Northey, and all three children started looking. 'Hm,' said Robert, some time later. 'We'll have to get up a bit earlier than usual if we're going to pay Mr Pearce a visit!'

Have a good look at the map. Can you find the road where Mr Pearce lives?

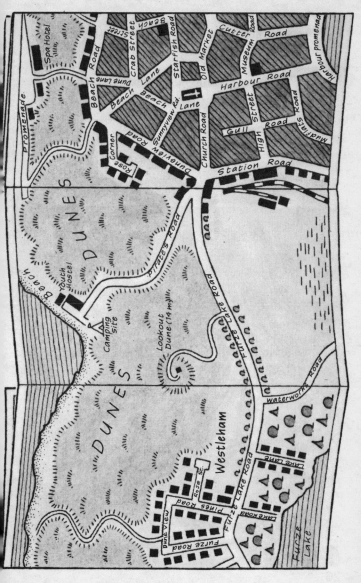

Spa Hotel

Promenade

Beach Road

Beach Lane

Dune Lane

Crab Street

Beach Street

Beach Lane

Sunnyview Rd.

Duneview Road

Starfish Road

Church Road

Old Market

Museum Road

Cutter Road

Harbour Road

Gull Street

High Street

Sunny Road

Mudflats

Harbour promenade

Rose Corner

Station Road

Pirate's Road

DUNES

Beach

Youth Hostel

Camping Site

Lookout Dune (14 m)

Furze Lake Road

Lake Road

Waterworks Road

DUNES

Westleham

Lake Lane

Furze Lake Road

Lake Road

Rose St.

Pines Road

Dune View Road

Furze Road

Furze Lake

11 All three children got dressed very early next morning. Robert wrote their parents a quick note, and then the three of them set off on the way to Westleham, a little village beside Furze Lake.

'Second turning on the right,' said Robert, when they reached the first houses of the village after about fifteen minutes' walk.

'Here we are – Number 12!' whispered Sandy, as if they might be overheard. 'Now what?'

'What do you think?' said Conker. 'We can't very well ring the bell – so we'll just have to wait and see if Henry Pearce is our H. Pearce.' They found a hiding place with a good view of the house, but nothing happened for quite a long time.

At last they heard the rattle of a bicycle chain behind the house, and then someone rode out of a side alley and into the village street on the now familiar bicycle. It was Pearce all right. The children were taken rather by surprise. 'I say, he's in a hurry this morning. Come on, after him!' said Conker.

'No use,' said Robert. 'He's got too big a start. But at least we know he's the right man.' They watched Pearce disappear down the road.

All of a sudden Sandy started running. 'Come on!' she cried. 'He's just lit a cigarette and thrown something into the bushes.'

They searched the rose bushes by the roadside carefully. 'Got it!' cried Conker triumphantly. 'Evidence at last – proof that our friend does smoke the smuggled cigarettes!'

 Try to find that important piece of evidence among the wild roses. What is it?

12 Conker held it up jubilantly. An empty cigarette packet – without any duty stamp on it. 'What a piece of luck!' breathed Robert, examining the crumpled packet. He smoothed it out as much as he could and put it between the pages of his notebook.

'Right,' said Conker, pleased. 'Now let's go back to his house. If anyone opens the door we'll say we left something at the kiosk yesterday.'

Robert and Sandy nodded.

Somebody did open the door when they rang – an elderly lady. Sandy asked politely if they could see Mr Pearce.

'Oh, I'm afraid you can't, not today,' said the old lady. 'The kiosk's closed – it's Mr Pearce's day off. He always goes shopping on the mainland on his day off.'

The three children looked at each other. They knew what they thought about that! Robert tapped his notebook, with the crumpled cigarette packet hidden

inside it.

'You could try again this afternoon,' the old lady suggested. 'He usually catches the three o' clock ferry home.'

'Want to bet he comes back with his cases full?' said Robert, as they hurried back along the road. 'He had them on the back of his bike when he left.'

'Yes – and we have plenty of time to convince the police they should investigate him,' said Conker, rather out of breath. 'We'll just go down to the harbour first, in case we're in time to see our friend leave.'

'We needn't bother,' said Sandy, slowing down. 'There's no point.'

 Can you tell why the children aren't in any hurry for the time being?

13 When they reached the first houses of Northey town, the ferry was well out to sea, just passing the shallow waters of the mudflats. 'I'm ravenous for breakfast, but let's go and have another look through Mr Gull's window first,' said Sandy. 'We can see if the case is still there.'

'Yes, it is,' said Conker a little later, and they left the back yard of the shop again and walked through the pedestrian precinct. There weren't many people about yet.

'Probably just a coincidence – it happens to be the same sort of case as Pearce's,' said Sandy.

'And I expect Mr Gull lends him that bike, not suspecting anything, because he lives so far from the town,' Robert added. 'It wouldn't be needed for delivering things in the evenings, after all.'

'Yes, that's about it,' agreed Conker, as they sat down to their breakfast at last, and told their father the full story.

'And if you hadn't stopped us following that man yesterday evening,' Robert told his father, reproachfully, 'we'd probably have found him fetching the bike from Mr Gull's shop.'

'Hm – and do you seriously think we're going to the police with you?' inquired Mr Williams thoughtfully.

'Oh, yes please!' begged Sandy. 'Let's go now!'

'There isn't even far to go,' said Conker suddenly, jumping up. 'And look, there's a policeman! If we hurry, we can tell him all about it here and now.'

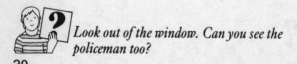
Look out of the window. Can you see the policeman too?

ROOM
TO LET

12

14 'Yes, I found that cat this morning, and the lady opposite was glad to have it back,' said the policeman, as he sat down at the breakfast table. 'I'm Sergeant Strong, by the way. Now, young people, your father said you had a story which might interest the police?'

'Yes, it's about that circular,' said Conker, getting his word in first. He pointed to the sideboard.

They spent the next half hour telling their story. Finally, Robert proudly showed the policeman the entries in his notebook, and the empty cigarette packet.

'Hm, yes, very interesting,' said Sergeant Strong. He looked at the time. 'Still more than four hours to go. Will you let me enlist the help of these young people at three this afternoon?' he asked Mr and Mrs Williams. They nodded. Robert, Sandy and Conker were delighted.

They met Sergeant Strong by the landing stage at three, and were soon pacing impatiently up and down.

The sergeant mopped his brow – it was a hot day. 'Here he comes!' cried Sandy, suddenly. But Pearce had obviously spotted Strong's police cap, because he swerved aside and vanished into the crowd for a moment. Then they saw him just about to get on his bicycle.

'Just a moment!' said the sergeant, sternly. 'Is your name Pearce?'

'Yes,' Pearce admitted.

'Then you're suspected of selling duty-free cigarettes on Northey Island,' said the policeman.

'Why, that's ridiculous!' said Pearce, angrily, and he tried to ride away.

'Got any luggage with you?' asked Sergeant Strong.

'No, of course not! You can see I haven't,' said Pearce.

'He's lying!' cried Sandy. 'He had two suitcases!'

 Have a good look around the crowd. Where are the two suitcases?

33

15 Pearce suddenly looked scared. 'You brat!' he shouted at Sandy, who stepped back in alarm.

'Now, now, take it easy,' said Sergeant Strong. 'The mere fact that you dumped those cases in the parcels van looks rather suspicious.'

Conker put the cases down in front of Strong. 'Are these cases your property?' Pearce said nothing.

'Anyone can see they are!' said Conker, pointing to the tags on the suitcases.

'Mr Pearce, I'm afraid I shall have to ask you to come to the police station with me,' said Sergeant Strong.

Sandy, Robert and Conker shouted for joy when the cases were opened at the police station. Pearce watched, looking very sour. Sergeant Strong shook his head as if he could hardly believe it. 'What a haul!' he said. 'Two cases full of duty-free cigarettes! Where did you get them?' But Pearce still didn't reply. 'Well, I'll just give the Customs and Excise office in Northport a call. They're going to be very interested in this!' said the sergeant, picking up a telephone.

'Line's engaged,' he said a moment later. 'Well then, you young, er – ace detectives! Can you tell me the whole story again in detail? We'll need your statement as evidence.' He looked gloomily at the typewriter in his office. He wasn't very fond of typing statements.

'Don't worry, we'll type it out for you!' said Sandy and Conker. But Robert's mind was on something else. He had fished a note out of a pouch inside the lid of one of the suitcases, and was turning the piece of paper this way and that. 'Just a moment, Sergeant Strong!' he said. 'Pearce did have an accomplice! Look – it's all in code!'

All those letters don't seem to make much sense. But some of them, read in the right order, give you a message. What is it?

16 When the police car drove up to The Dunes boarding house late that afternoon, there was steaming hot chocolate ready for the three children. 'Here are your Ace Detectives back,' said Sergeant Strong, grinning. Then he told the children's parents everything that had happened.

'Really quick off the mark, your kids!' he finished.

'You forgot to say Pearce had an accomplice,' Sandy reminded him.

'So I did!' said Sergeant Strong, glancing at Robert. 'Yes, Robert here found a note inside the case. And what do you think it says? "Final delivery. They are on our trail. Captain." To cut a long story short, the idea of smuggling cigarettes came from the ferry captain, who was allowed to buy stocks of duty-free tobacco for his ship. Our colleagues in Northport will have a warm welcome waiting for him this evening!'

Mr and Mrs Williams wanted to know all the details, and it was almost an hour before Sergeant Strong was able to leave. Robert pushed his notebook across the table as the sergeant rose to his feet. 'I've just been making up a secret alphabet,' he told the policeman. 'You must solve this coded message before you go!'

Sergeant Strong looked puzzled, but everyone else glanced at him expectantly. 'All right, then!' he said, laughing. 'Hand it over!' No one said anything for two minutes, and then the sergeant put his pencil down.

'Well done!' he said. 'And I expect I *will* be seeing you three again before too long!'

Look carefully at the secret message. Using Robert's key, you can easily decode it. What does it say?

anchor A
buoy B
camp C
dunes D
eel E
fish F
gull G
harpoon H
island I
jellyfish J
kiosk K
lighthouse L

mussel M
net N
octopus O
periscope P
quay Q
rope R
starfish S
turtle T
U boat U
volcano V
waves W
yacht Y

XZ

An Almost Perfect Robbery

1 It was a beautiful afternoon, and the children were down by the sea. Conker and Sandy were playing beach tennis, while Robert dozed in the sun. 'I'm bored!' he moaned, fishing out his notebook from under the *Island News*. He opened it at the page with the secret alphabet. The last entry in the notebook said, in code, 'See you again soon. The Ace Detectives.'

'It's about time something happened!' Robert said, but Conker and Sandy took no notice. So he went on looking at the newspaper and feeling bored.

Suddenly a headline caught his eye. 'Thieving Magpies in Seaview Hotel.' Robert quickly skimmed through the news story. Then he jumped up excitedly, to show Sandy and Conker what he had been reading.

'Hm,' said Conker thoughtfully. 'You wouldn't have thought so many silver spoons and knives and forks could just disappear! It's funny they didn't find a single clue in the attic mentioned here.'

SEAVIEW

Greetings from Northey

'Perhaps we could help!' suggested Sandy.

'Just what I was thinking myself,' agreed Robert. He pulled his T-shirt on and put the notebook away.

The Seaview Hotel was quite an old building, dating from the last century. The lady at the reception desk was doubtful at first when Conker said they wanted to see the proprietor, but then she picked up the telephone. Sandy was impatiently twirling the picture postcard stand. Suddenly she took a card off it. 'I say – something about the hotel has changed!' she said. 'This is really rather interesting!'

 Have a look at the old picture of the hotel. Compare it with the hotel today. What is the difference?

2 'Well, well!' said Robert. 'So there was once a big tree outside the hotel, with a stout branch sticking out right in front of one of the attic windows. I wonder ...'

'Hullo – did you want to see me?' asked an elderly gentleman. 'My name's Mr Benedict. I'm the proprietor.'

'Oh, Mr Benedict,' said Sandy, very politely, 'we heard about the disappearance of your family silver, and we thought ...'

Mr Benedict laughed. 'Ah, I see! Sergeant Strong's already warned me! You must be the Ace Detectives. And I suppose you're on the trail already!'

'Well, we might be!' said Robert seriously. He showed Mr Benedict the postcard. 'Is that big branch in front of the attic room where the silver was kept?'

Mr Benedict nodded. 'Yes, but why do you ask?'

'The tree isn't there now,' said Sandy. 'When was it chopped down?'

'Last March,' said Mr Benedict.

Conker thought hard. 'Was that window ever broken?'

Mr Benedict frowned thoughtfully, and said, 'So you think the silver may have been stolen while the tree still stood there? And the thief got in by way of the branch?' The Ace Detectives nodded. Mr Benedict shook his head doubtfully. 'Come into my office,' he said. 'Well, yes, the window actually was broken early this year, when there was a fierce storm. You should have seen the damage! I took photographs next morning, to show the insurance company.' He looked in a desk drawer, and found a photograph.

Conker examined it closely, and then said, 'Have you lost anything else, Mr Benedict?'

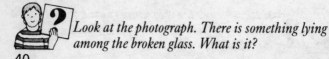

Look at the photograph. There is something lying among the broken glass. What is it?

40

3 'You mean a button? No, children, that kind of button's only found on seamen's jackets,' said Mr Benedict. 'I don't have a jacket like that.'

Robert had a look at the photograph too. 'This could mean someone got in through the window and lost a button in the process.'

'Could we see the room in the attic?' asked Sandy.

'Whatever for, children?' said Mr Benedict. 'I can assure you, Sergeant Strong searched it for clues, and he didn't find a thing!' However, looking at the children's hopeful faces, he added, 'Oh, very well, then! But I must go to the reception desk and get the key first.'

'Don't you have a private key to the room, if it contained all that silver?' asked Sandy.

'I never needed one before,' said Mr Benedict. 'Last year we were still letting it as a bedroom. Then we had some alterations done in the winter and turned that part of the attic into a boxroom.'

'And when was the chest of silver taken up there?' asked Robert.

'After Christmas. That's when I last saw it,' said Mr Benedict. 'We still call the room Number 18, out of habit.' There was a little boy standing by the big board of keys at the reception desk. 'Oh no!' groaned Mr Benedict. 'My grandson's been mixing all the keys up again!' The Ace Detectives grinned at each other. 'I can't see 18 anywhere!' he added, looking baffled.

'It's all right,' said Robert, going up to the board. 'There's the key!'

Have you found it too? Look closely at the keys – only one can be Number 18. Which is it?

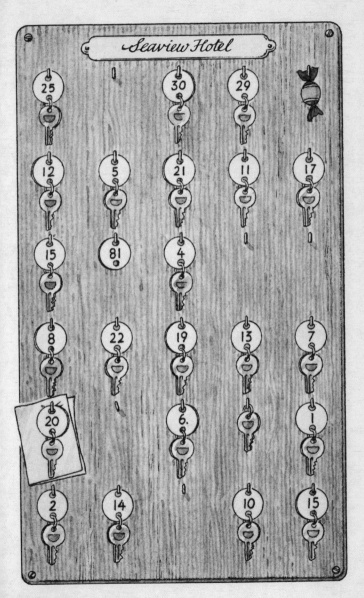

4 'That little imp!' said Mr Benedict crossly. Then he put the tag saying 18 back on the key which had been hanging under Number 13.

It was hot and stuffy in the attic room. Mr Benedict opened the window, and Robert leaned out and looked down. 'There's the tree stump,' he murmured, opening his notebook to make a little sketch of it.

After the children had had a good look round, Conker asked, 'Could we borrow that photograph?'

'If you like!' said Mr Benedict, smiling. He locked the door again.

'Not a trace of a clue,' said Sandy, as they left the hotel.

'What I don't understand is the fact that obviously anyone could have got into the room,' said Conker.

'You're right,' agreed Sandy. 'The thief didn't need to come through the window – '

' – and lose that button!' Robert added, tapping the photograph.

'Mr Benedict noticed that the silver was missing only three days ago,' said Conker thoughtfully. 'But it could have been gone as long as four or five months!'

'Yes,' muttered Robert.

'Listen – we must go straight back!' said Conker suddenly.

'Why?' asked Robert.

'It may be a help to know just when the storm was when the window was broken,' Conker explained.

'I don't think we need to go back,' said Sandy. Robert and Conker looked at her in surprise. She had stopped in front of a photgrapher's window and was looking at all the pictures displayed in a case. 'We can find the date here!'

 Look hard at all the photographs. You will find the date of the storm on one of them. Which one?

44

PHOTOGRAPHER

STARFISH

Prints,
Nos. 17-24,
50p. each

BEACH

WE MAKE
THE BEST
OF YOUR
PHOTOS!

SPA HOTEL

Ship grounded
after storm
13 Feb. 1899

Souvenirs
of your stay in
Northey,
50p each

Saturday
assistant
wanted!

5 'Ship grounded after storm, 13 February this year,' Robert read out. The photograph showed a beached ship tilting to one side.

Sandy did some sums, and said, 'So if that was really the day the silver disappeared, as we think, the thief's already had a hundred and thirty-eight days to cover up his tracks!'

Conker shook his head gloomily, and Robert groaned. 'Yes, it was a great stroke of luck for him that Mr Benedict didn't look for it sooner!' he said.

Several days passed by before the Ace Detectives had a stroke of luck themselves. The Williams family were all on their way back from the beach, and Robert was well ahead of the others when he noticed a tourist office poster, advertising some of the things you could do on Northey Island. 'I say – the old sailor here is wearing a jacket with a button missing!' he muttered to himself, hastily reading the words under the picture. Then he tore a page out of his notebook and wrote a secret message. He speared it on the twig of a bush, at about eye-level, and then ran off.

'Where's Robert?' asked Sandy, looking up and down the road.

'Look – something must have happened!' Conker told her, taking the note off the twig, and he quickly read the coded message. 'He must have another clue!' he said, giving his parents his bathing things. 'Come on, Sandy – let's go and meet Robert and find out what he knows!'

 Look up the key to the secret code from the Ace Detectives' last adventure. What does the coded message say?

6 'On the trail. Meet at Neptune's Fountain,' shouted Conker, as he and Sandy ran down the road. But when they reached the fountain, they had to wait almost ten minutes before Robert turned up.

'Ah, at last!' said Sandy, when he finally appeared.

'What's up?' asked Conker, impatiently.

Robert told them what he had seen on the poster. 'And they told me at the tourist office that old Harry Hodgson used to be the keeper of the West Lighthouse. He's retired now, but he still lives in the lighthouse, and he takes tourists round the mudflats once a week.'

As soon as the children had had lunch, they hired bicycles and cycled over the island to the West Lighthouse. The old lighthouse keeper was busy in his garden when they arrived.

'Hullo, Mr Hodgson,' said Sandy. 'The tourist office told us we could see over the tower.'

Mr Hodgson looked at the children. 'Well, they usually let me know beforehand,' he said, puffing at his pipe. 'But come along in! I suppose they told you you'd have to look round on your own? I can't go with you.'

'Why not?' asked Conker.

'On account of all the steps,' explained Mr Hodgson. 'I can't get all that way up, not nowadays.'

'Then who looks after the light?' asked Robert.

'It's all done automatically these days,' snorted Mr Hodgson, as if he didn't think much of things that worked automatically. 'Someone comes over from the mainland now and then to service the light.'

'Yes, he comes every fortnight, and he likes prawns!' said Sandy.

 How could Sandy tell? Look around the room for the clue she spotted.

MIND THE
STEPS

Joe service
Mudflats
Bingo

Mudflats

Joe
service

Prawn
for
Joe

R

7 Mr Hodgson quite forgot to puff at his pipe for a moment. 'However did you know?' he asked.

Sandy pointed to the calendar on the wall by the grandfather clock. 'It says so there!' she said.

'Can we climb up the lighthouse now?' asked Robert, and Mr Hodgson nodded.

The light itself was in a room with big glass windows at the top of the tower, and the Ace Detectives were quite out of breath when they got there. 'Two hundred and seventy-seven steps!' panted Sandy.

'At least it can't have been the lighthouse keeper who climbed that tree outside the Seaview Hotel,' said Conker. 'He's too old!'

'I'm afraid we're on the wrong track,' said Robert. 'All the same, once we get down again we must see if we can get a look at that seaman's jacket. I want to find out if it really does have a missing button.'

'Not a bad view over the island, eh?' said Mr Hodgson, when they came running down the steps again. 'Did you three know that the halogen light up there can be seen over the water for a distance of twenty-three nautical miles?' The Ace Detectives said they didn't.

'What's that over there?' asked Sandy, changing the subject. She was standing by the window, shielding her eyes with her hand as she peered out. Mr Hodgson and Conker went over.

'Oh, that! That's the old ruin,' said Mr Hodgson. 'The gulls like to nest there, and . . . ' He went on talking about the old ruin, and meanwhile Robert had a chance to look round for the jacket. 'I've found the jacket!' he told Conker in a whisper. 'There it is!'

The jacket is hanging up somewhere, half hidden – can you tell where by looking round the room?

8 The jacket was reflected in a mirror in the next room. Conker got the message and guided the old lighthouse keeper over to a big map of the island, saying he'd like to know about the different places. The two of them had their backs to Robert, who quickly and quietly darted into the other room. He came back just as quietly, perspiring slightly, and went to look at the map as well.

'Is that your son?' he asked, pointing to a photograph pinned up beside the map.

'Oh no!' said Mr Hodgson. 'That's the potter – my neighbour. His house is over there by Furze Lake.'

'Was the picture taken at a Christmas party?' asked Conker.

Mr Hodgson grinned, puffing at his pipe. 'Well, not exactly, children. That was the opening of his pottery.'

'It looks as if he borrowed your jacket, did he?' inquired Robert.

'That's right – he wanted to go out and buy some food

52

and drink, because it was running out,' said Mr Hodgson. 'Terrible weather it was that day! He came back soaked!'

Robert was suddenly in a great hurry, and said they must go. 'Come and see me again some time,' the lighthouse keeper called, as they mounted their bicycles.

'My goodness!' said Robert excitedly, as they rode away. 'The potter was wearing that jacket!'

'And did the button really come off it?' asked Sandy.

Robert nodded. 'Yes, it's a perfect match! There's a piece of fabric torn off the jacket too.'

All was still outside the pottery. 'I'm afraid it's not open,' said Conker. 'Early closing!' He tried the door several times. 'I say – hold on!' he suddenly cried. 'Here's a name we know!'

 You know the name too. Have you found it yet? What is it?

53

9 Robert let out a long whistle. He had found the name as well! 'B. Benedict. Pottery,' said the notice on the door. 'Can he be related to Mr Benedict of the Seaview Hotel?' he wondered.

Conker was going to say something, when Sandy called out, 'And he makes silver jewellery too – it says so here!' She pointed to another notice, which could only just be seen in the darkness of the room.

'I think we ought to go and see Sergeant Strong,' suggested Conker. 'We aren't going to get any farther here, not today.'

'Yes, and then let's go to the Seaview Hotel and ask Mr Benedict what he knows about this pottery,' said Robert.

'Not much, I'm afraid,' was Mr Benedict's answer, as they sat in his office later, along with Sergeant Strong. 'Yes, the place down by the lake belongs to my son. He took it into his head to turn that old fisherman's cottage into a pottery. We had quite a quarrel over it. He wanted money to convert the place, and I wouldn't let him have it. He hasn't set foot in my house since!'

Sergeant Strong was looking thoughtful. Mr Benedict paused for a moment, and then went on.

'They say his opening was a big success, though. I kept this little news item from the *Island News*.' He rummaged in a drawer again, and found it. 'Only because it mentioned my hotel,' he said, rather apologetically, pointing to the place where they could read the words 'Seaview Hotel'.

Sergeant Strong and the Ace Detectives studied the news item carefully. Suddenly Robert said, 'I say, I've seen the light! Read it again!'

Read the news story carefully yourself. You will find a date that you've met before. What is it?

54

...ipping
...ps, which
...thouse of
...ce stone
...he cliffs
...from the
...and west.

Gravesend to Northey Island when a
storm blew up an the ship had to seek
shelter.

...lar

...ws

...rmen's
...00 tons a
...where the
...nchored
...harbour.
...e
...it

Island Pottery Opened

NORTHEY ISLAND — The first
pottery on Northey Island opened
yesterday, with a small party for
friends and invited guests.

Brian Benedict, son of the proprietor
of the Seaview Hotel, welcomed over a
hundred guests to his pottery, despite
the stormy weather. The pleasant
rooms in his house by Furze Lake have
been tastefully renovated, and besides
the pottery made by Brian himself,
silver jewellery of his own design and
antiques are on sale.

The fact that yesterday was Friday,
13 February didn't seem to worry Brian
Benedict. He gave our reporter to
understand that he is not superstitious.

10 '13 February!' said Conker, slapping his knee. 'What about it?' asked Sergeant Strong.

'The big storm was on 13 February!' explained Robert.

'And one of Mr Benedict's attic windows was broken that night,' Sandy went on.

'And you can see a button on the window sill,' said Conker, pointing to the photograph.

'A button belonging to the old lighthouse keeper's jacket,' Robert added.

'The one he lent young Mr Benedict on the night of his opening party, on the night of 13 February. Mr Hodgson told us he borrowed it to go out to get some more food and drink,' Sandy finished.

Mr Benedict went quite pale. 'You ... you don't mean to say ... ' he stammered.

Sergeant Strong looked thoughtful. 'That's what might have happened,' he said rather unhappily. 'Well,

we'll be off to Furze Lake first thing tomorrow!'

Next day, Sergeant Strong told the potter why he suspected him. 'Can you show me any receipts for the purchase of the silver you use for making jewellery?' he asked. Brian Benedict hesitated.

'Here's the lighthouse keeper's jacket!' said the police constable who had come with them. He had been to see Mr Hodgson and borrow it. Robert handed Sergeant

Strong the photograph. 'Yes,' said the sergeant, 'it all fits! The button really does seem to be off this jacket. Mr Benedict, have you ever worn it?'

Brian Benedict shook his head. 'That's not true!' cried Sandy angrily. 'He did wear it, at least once! And he knows that too, because he has a copy of the same photograph we saw at the lighthouse!'

The photograph is hidden somewhere in the room. Can you see it?

11 'Goodness me!' said the sergeant in amazement. 'How on earth did you discover that photograph?'

'Well, we've seen it before,' said Robert, 'so we could recognize it even half hidden in that pile of books!'

'Mr Benedict, I'm afraid you've got a little explaining to do,' said Sergeant Strong, pulling out a chair for himself. 'On Friday the 13th, were you...'

'Here!' whispered Conker, beckoning the others over. 'There's still one piece of the jigsaw missing,' he told them thoughtfully.

'Yes – how did he transport the silver?' wondered Robert.

They were sitting outside the pottery in the warm morning sunlight. 'And how did he get it down the tree in such a storm?' asked Sandy.

They walked round the house, and took a closer look at a tumbledown shed. After quite a while, they found what

SILVER MAG
Refreshing beer

MAGPIE
BREWERIE

they were after. 'What about this, then?' asked Sandy, pulling a large and grubby rucksack out of the junk in the shed. 'There are a couple of ropes here, too!'

'The stuff's been lying in here for quite a while, by the look of it,' said Conker.

'But he could have let the heavy rucksack down with the help of those ropes,' said Robert, working it out. 'I think we'd better show these to Sergeant Strong.'

Suddenly there was a scurrying noise as a mouse ran across the shed. 'Stop!' cried Conker, all of a sudden.

'The mouse won't stop for you!' said Sandy.

'Don't be silly! It showed me something, though!' And Conker couldn't help roaring with laughter. 'You have a look too, and see if I'm not right!'

It's easy enough to lose things in a pile of junk — but there's something important here. It might be the final proof. What is it?

59

12 'A fork!' said Robert, picking it up from where it lay behind a rusty old tin advertising poster.

'Real silver!' said Conker. 'But of course, only old Mr Benedict can say whether it's part of the stolen cutlery.'

Sergeant Strong was still busy with Brian Benedict when the Ace Detectives came racing into the room, shouting with triumph. 'Perhaps this will help you, Sergeant!' said Sandy, holding up the fork.

'My word!' said the surprised sergeant. 'Wherever did you find that?'

'In the shed,' said Sandy. 'A mouse and a magpie showed us this fork!'

Sergeant Strong didn't understand, but he said sternly, 'Well, Mr Benedict, was this part of your father's silver?'

The potter nodded, slowly. Sergeant Strong went into the next room. 'I've just called the Seaview Hotel,' he said, when he came back. 'You should be grateful to your father, Mr Benedict. He says he won't lay any charges against you. And as for you Ace Detectives, Mr Benedict has a surprise for you at the hotel. Come with me!'

So later that afternoon, they all gathered in Mr Benedict's office. 'Well, now,' said Mr Benedict, clearing his throat. 'In short – since you three solved the mystery of the missing silver, there's a reward for you!' The Ace Detectives beamed. 'But seeing you're detectives, you'll have to puzzle out what it is!' added Mr Benedict, laughing. 'There's something hidden in this room – you'll find out what it is if you can read this coded message,' Mr Benedict went on, holding up a piece of paper.

Robert took a look at the paper, and then said happily, 'What a splendid surprise!'

*Write the decoded message in the little boxes –
what does it say?*

60

13 'An instant camera!' cried the children, when they had found it hidden on top of the china cupboard. 'Great!' They thanked Mr Benedict very much.

'That's all right, children,' said Mr Benedict. 'You must thank your parents too – they say they'll give you film to use in it now and then!'

They had tea, with delicious cakes, and the cheerful party went on for almost two hours as they discussed the case of the almost perfect robbery, and Conker took the first photographs. The camera whirred and produced its photographs several times that afternoon.

'Please keep these as a souvenir!' said Sandy, putting the pictures on the table.

'That reminds me!' said Sergeant Strong suddenly. 'I almost forgot!' And he brought a small black notebook with red corners out of a pocket of his jacket. 'Here, Robert, this is for you! The holidays aren't over yet – and who knows? You may need to make notes on other mysterious cases!'

Now that you're a trained detective, you'll have noticed that the wings of the seagull on the right-hand pages are not in the same position each time. Close the book and then ruffle through it with your right thumb. What do you see? A moving picture – the seagull is flying, bringing you greetings from Northey Island!